Life in the Arctic with
Nina & Nikita

written by

Julie Ewashen

Illustrations by Nadine Riehl

ISBN
978-1-4602-2727-5 (Paperback)
978-1-4602-2728-2 (eBook)

Produced by:

FriesenPress

Suite 300 – 852 Fort Street
Victoria, BC, Canada V8W 1H8

www.friesenpress.com

Distributed to the trade by The Ingram Book Company

Foreword

For me, stories evoke memories of long winter evenings by the fire, a mother who made clothes for my beloved dolls, and a father who always obliged when a child pleaded, "Tell me a story."

I am indebted to Norbert Rosing, whose wonderful photographs of a polar bear playing with an Alaskan Husky sled dog inspired me, and led to further research.

Financial assistance towards the cost of illustrations from Columbia — Kootenay Cultural Alliance is gratefully acknowledged.

Appreciation is extended to Doctor Luanne Armstrong for her editing and encouragement.

Thanks to Eileen Delman, who initially donated time for copy editing and positive reviews, and to my final editor at Friesen Press for practical suggestions and warm praise.

Heartfelt thanks to all who have read a work in progress and provided insights.

Appreciation is extended to my husband, children, grandchildren, and extended family, for everything.

Sincerely,
Julie Ewashen.

Part One

Momma
— **Polar Bear** —

Momma Polar Bear lived in Alaska, near the Arctic Ocean. One day she was walking on the tundra, sniffing the air. She followed her nose and eventually reached a dead whale that was lying on the beach.

She was very hungry, so she began to eat. Suddenly, she stopped and sniffed the air again; she was pretty sure she smelled a Daddy polar bear.

Momma knew he would be twice her size, and that he would be much stronger. What if he pushed her away and stole her food?

With this thought, she began to eat faster.

The Daddy bear appeared. He began to eat the whale near the tail. Momma was eating near the head. She looked at him and growled. He stopped eating for a moment, and gave her a loving look.

By the time the bears finished eating, it was late evening, and the Northern Lights had painted the skies with many beautiful colours.

The two of them washed their paws and their faces. Then, Daddy Bear noticed that Momma Bear still had a dirty spot on her face.

Gently, he licked it off.

Daddy Bear and Momma Bear stayed together for several days. Then Daddy said goodbye and left to search for food.

New cubs were beginning to grow inside Momma Bear.

She went to the Arctic Ocean and found two big holes in the ice.

She caught a lot of fish there and ate them. Then she smelled seal, her favourite food. She swam under water until she reached the seals' breathing hole. She caught two and ate them. Over time, Momma continued to catch seal and fish. She ate as much as she could, and she grew quite fat.

One day, she walked near the beach, looking for a big snow drift. When she found one as big as a house, she stopped. She dug into the snow with her sharp front claws and used her hind legs to push the snow into place. After a lot of hard work, her snow cave, which would be her den, had three walls and a roof.

The Northern Lights were glowing, and the stars were shining bright as Momma stood outside. She looked at the world around her.

After a few moments, she went inside her den. She used her back legs to push snow in front of the entrance. Now she had a door. The den would freeze solid and she would stay safe.

Momma wore a thick white coat with shades of yellow. It was lined with lots of fat to keep her warm.

She lay down for an extra-long sleep; it was time to hibernate. She would sleep through the winter, and she would not need to eat or drink.

In the middle of winter, Momma Bear gave birth to twin cubs. One was Nina, a female, the other was Nikita, a male. The cubs' eyes were shut tight, and they could not see. Although they had ears, they could not hear.

There was a nasty blizzard outside. The cubs had almost no fur, and snuggled up to Momma Bear to keep warm. She was half asleep and half awake.

The cubs were smaller than a tiny Chihuahua dog, or a kitten that was one month old.

They drank their mother's sweet, creamy milk, and they had naps.

Spring began when the cubs were ten weeks old. Now they could see and hear, and they were covered with smooth white fur.

Momma Bear finally woke right up and looked around her den. She went to the snow door and pushed it open with her nose. Then she walked outside and sniffed to make sure all was safe. The cubs followed and stayed close beside her.

Part Two
— Nikita & Nina —

The polar bear cubs left their den with Momma Bear.

Nina rolled on to her back while Nikita stood still and looked at the world. The world looked very big and scary.

Soon, the twins got used to being outside and began to find it exciting. They felt safe when they were close to their Momma.

They enjoyed the warmth from her nice thick coat.

At night, the three bears returned to the den to sleep.

After a few days, Momma decided that it was time for the cubs to learn how to climb over a snowdrift. The pads of fur on their feet would keep them warm and stop them from slipping.

Momma went to the top and encouraged the twins to come to her.

Halfway from the bottom, on the other side of the drift, Nina tumbled in the snow. Nikita tumbled after her.

They both laughed as they rolled over and over in the soft, white snow.

Later, just as they were dozing off, an Arctic hare ran in front of them. Momma ran after the hare, and the twins ran after Momma.

Nikita tripped and fell. Then Nina fell on top of Nikita. They both laughed as they rolled over in the snow.

Momma did not want to leave her cubs alone. She stopped running, and the hare escaped.

Now Momma was feeling hungry. She thought about how good that hare would have tasted, and she felt even more hungry.

Then she looked at her cubs having fun. *How lucky I am*, she thought. *They are such beautiful cubs!*

The sky was a light purple when Nina decided she needed some of her mother's milk.

Nikita wagged his tail as he followed Nina. He was thinking how Momma's milk was sweet like honey.

Momma stood while they both had a drink.

When they finished, Momma told her cubs it was time to go fishing.

"I want to sleep," said Nina.

"I want to fish," said Nikita.

"I need to eat," said Momma. "I have to have food to make milk for you to drink."

The cubs did not want to be without Momma's yummy milk.

They walked out on the frozen sea as evening fell.

Momma found an ice hole and they sat beside it.

It was getting dark when a seal poked its head out. Quick as a wink, Momma grabbed it with her mouth.

She turned around to share it with her cubs — but only Nikita was there. He liked the smell of the seal and he wanted to eat.

"No," said Momma, "You stay with the food while I look for Nina."

Momma stood and sniffed,
trying to pick up Nina's scent.

She soon found her — fast
asleep under the stars.
Momma smiled as she gently
nudged her.

Nina did not want to wake
up. Momma told her that Nikita
was guarding a late-night treat.

Momma Bear and Nina returned to Nikita, and the three bears shared their food. Then the cubs nursed again, drinking Momma's milk.

Nikita gave Momma a goodnight kiss by nibbling her forehead.

Nina gave Momma a goodnight kiss by nibbling under her ear.

Nina and Nikita snuggled close to Momma, and the three bears went to sleep.

Part Three

— **Nina** —

Both of the twins grew quickly, but Nikita grew faster than Nina.

When he was six months old, he was as big as a large bulldog.

He liked to make himself look even bigger by standing on his hind legs.

Nina thought this was kind of silly.

When the cubs were two years old, they could find their own food and care for themselves. They were as grown up as a young human that is ready to graduate from high school.

Nikita was spending a lot of time with his friends. They often had play fights together.

One day, Nikita said goodbye to Momma and Nina, and went away with his friends.

Momma sat for a while, and then she went for a walk.

Nina sat thinking about her brother. She felt sad.

She had no one to play with.

She was wondering what to do when she heard a loud whirring sound overhead. It was a small airplane.

A shot rang out.

Nina did not like the loud noise.

She ran towards the ocean. Once there, she swam away as fast as she could.

Her white fur blended with the ice and snow on the Arctic Ocean. It would be hard for the men in the airplane to see her.

Nina was a strong swimmer, and she listened for the whirring noise as she swam. When she could no longer hear the noise, she looked for an iceberg on which to sit.

She gripped it with her sharp claws. The furry pads on her feet stopped her from slipping as she climbed aboard.

When she had travelled a long way, she began to feel hungry.

She stood up and looked in the water. She saw lots of fish, but she didn't see any seal (which was her favourite). Fish would have to do.

She went in the water and caught a fish in her big mouth. Then she returned to her trusty boat, and ate the fish.

Nina swam towards a bigger ice floe and climbed abroad. This one was very comfortable, and it moved swiftly through the water.

Days and nights passed Nina went in the water to fish. Each time, she returned to her iceberg to eat.

Sometimes she slept.

More days and nights passed.

Winds and ocean currents moved the ice floe along quickly.

Still more days and nights passed.

THEN...

The ice floe reached the Atlantic Ocean!

Nina had travelled a long, long, long way. She could see the Canadian coastline!

At Hudson Bay, Nina decided to swim ashore. Once on land, she lay down and rested in the sun.

She was almost asleep when she smelled an Arctic hare.

It was running right in front of her!

Nina gave chase. She wanted a change from seafood.

Part Four

— Nina's Paw —

Nigel's mom was away: he was traveling in a truck with his dad, whose name was John, and his Alaskan Husky sled dog, Fido.

Suddenly, John slowed the truck and stopped.

Nigel saw an Arctic hare — a big white rabbit — run across the road. A large white shadow followed. Excitedly, Nigel yelled, "Look Dad! A polar bear is chasing the hare!"

"I bet the bear catches the hare!" Nigel continued. "Let's call her 'Nina' after Mom!

She is not big enough to be a Daddy bear. Look! She is —"

Nigel gasped as Nina suddenly fell down. She lay very still. Something was sticking out of her right front paw. The paw was bleeding — bleeding a lot.

"Dad! Can't we stop the bleeding? She might die!"

"You're right, son — but first we'll have to tranquilize her."

John put a tranquilizer into his dart gun.

He loaded the dart into his rifle and aimed it at Nina's right rear hip.

Then he took a special collar and pen from his bag. He wrote the date and the place — *Churchill, Manitoba* — on the collar.

"Dad, I'm a pretty neat printer. Let me do her name."

John passed him the collar. Nigel printed *Nina* and gave the collar back to his dad.

John walked to Nina and pushed on her back with his foot.

The bear lay still. Her wound was still bleeding. A piece of round steel could be seen through the bleeding.

John injected a local anesthetic, waited a few moments, then carefully pulled the steel out.

Nigel mopped up the blood, and they both saw two more steel pieces in the injured paw.

"I'll need the artery forceps to grab these," said John. Nigel passed the forceps, and John removed the other steel pieces. The wound bled more than ever.

Nigel held Nina's paw while John covered the wound with a dressing and a bandage.

John lifted the bear's head, and Nigel fastened her collar around her neck.

An artery forceps looks much like a scissors but it does not cut. It is made to grip tightly.

"Dad, can I get Fido?"

"Okay—but make sure he behaves."

Nigel opened the truck door.

"Fido, come! Meet a new friend. Heel!"

Nigel walked to Nina, and Fido followed.

Nigel stroked her. "Nina! Nina! Nina!" he repeated. Fido sniffed the bandage on Nina's sore foot. Then he sniffed along her leg and up towards her face. He nuzzled her fur. Nigel patted him and said, "Good dog!" As they were driving home, Nigel grabbed a rag and cleaned off the three pieces of steel which had been removed from Nina's paw.

"Look, Dad! These are bits from your electric drill!"

"That can't be," his dad answered. "I always put them away when I finish using them."

"I think you missed some after you worked on that post last week. This one is marked 3/8, this one 5/8, and the big one is 5/6. The big one is the one you pulled out first. The other two were further into the paw."

The more John thought about it, the more he realized that Nigel was on to something. "You're right!" he said. "I remember now—I stuck them into the ground, and I put them with the sharp ends facing up. That was a dangerous mistake! How could I have done that? I'm an animal lover and a biologist, so I should have known better. If someone else had done the same thing, I'd sure let them know about it."

"We all make mistakes, Dad," said Nigel. "It's okay—Nina's paw is going to get better."

Drill Bits In These Sizes Have Very Sharp V Shaped Tips On the end.

When they arrived home they loaded the truck with meat and water.

They took this to Nina and placed it near her.

Fido wanted to eat the meat.

"No!" said Nigel.

He had trained Fido well, and the dog obeyed.

After supper, Nigel went to bed, and Fido went to his dog house.

Early the next morning, Nigel called Fido, but he didn't come.

Nigel and his dad ate breakfast quickly and drove back to Nina.

Fido came running from behind a snowdrift. He had spent the night guarding Nina! She was weak from pain and loss of blood, and hadn't even touched her food.

Back home, Nigel said, "Dad, you know that salmon Uncle Peter brought? I was wondering... could I have a couple for Nina?"

"What? Uncle Peter brought those all the way from Winnipeg! Anyway, you know that what polar bears really like is seal."

"But we don't have any seal. Please, Dad! I'll help clean them."

"Well, okay. Let's get started. But don't be disappointed if Nina won't eat them. And who said you could borrow my green sweater?"

Nigel grinned a bit sheepishly. He was big for his thirteen years, and some of his dad's clothes fit him already. "I was cold, and your sweater was handy," he replied.

His dad laughed. "I see!" he said with a smile.

While they were cleaning the fish, Nigel threw a salmon to Fido.

"Go! Nina!" he said.

Fido caught the salmon in his mouth and ran to Nina.

He dropped it in front of her and wagged his tail.

Nina sniffed it, ate a little, and went to sleep.

Snow was falling before it was daylight the next morning. There was lots of snow where Nigel lived. He and his family lived in Churchill, which is a little town in a province called Manitoba, in a big country called Canada.

Pretend that you have three boxes and that you want to fit them into one another. Canada is great big box, Manitoba is a medium-sized box, and Churchill is a small box.

Fido stood at the door of the house and barked.

Soon Nigel came out and threw him a salmon, saying, "Go! Nina!"

Fido caught the salmon in his mouth and ran down the road to Nina.

Nina was standing on three feet and was holding up her sore paw when Fido brought her the fish.

The next evening, Nina stood on all four feet to eat and have a drink of water.

John and Nigel came by.

"Look, Dad!" Nigel said. "Nina is better!"

The next day, Nina wanted to play with Fido.

"Look, Dad! They are going to play together!"

"It sure looks like it. Too bad we can't take a picture. People won't believe it. I can hardly believe it myself!"

The sun was setting when Nina stood up and cuddled Fido. She held him between her chin and chest as she lifted him up and carried him around.

The stars were shining when she put Fido down. He reached up and licked her face.

Nigel smiled. "My dog is special," he said.

"Yes," said his Dad. "Nina is special too. Most bears would rather kill a dog than play with it."

Nina and Fido played together for several more days.

Other polar bears were going where it was colder — to places where there were more seals to hunt. Nina needed to go there too, so she could stock up on food before winter.

Nigel and Fido watched as she slowly walked away.

Perhaps Nina was wishing she could stay.

Nigel saw Fido wag his tail as Nina left — but he wagged it slowly and he looked sad.

That night Nigel had a dream:

Fido was thinking of Nina and her soft warm fur. Nina was wishing Fido could bring her salmon. They were playing together.

Nigel was already a very smart biologist. He planned to teach people that a polar bear and a Husky sled dog could be friends.

The END

About the Author

Author Julie Ewashen, maiden name O'Neill, is (like George Bernard Shaw), a graduate of Wesley College, Dublin, Ireland, where she was encouraged to pursue a career in writing. A retired registered nurse and midwife, she lives with her husband in Creston, B.C. Julie has studied creative writing by correspondence and workshops. She is a retired drama critic and reporter for the Creston Valley Advance and recently celebrated her eighty-first birthday

About the Illustrator

Illustrator Nadine Riehl is a graduate of Concordia University, Montreal, Quebec, where she received a B.A. in Fine Arts and Major in Studio Arts. Nadine acquired local fame when she painted her first mural in 2008 while on vacation from Kwantlen Polytech University, B.C. She lives on a farm in Creston Valley B.C., with her husband and son.